Close E...

An Erotic Adventure In Which
You Are The Hero

ALINA REYES

translated by
DAVID WATSON

A Phoenix Paperback

Derrière la Porte first published in 1994 by
Editions Robert Laffont, Paris

First published in Great Britain as
Behind Closed Doors by Alina Reyes
by Weidenfeld & Nicolson 1995

This abridged edition published in 1996 by Phoenix
a division of Orion Books Ltd
Orion House, 5 Upper St Martin's Lane, London WC2H 9EA

ISBN 1 85799 579 1

Typeset by Datix International Ltd, Bungay, Suffolk
Printed in Great Britain by Clays Ltd, St Ives plc

Contents

I

The Angels

As I reached the door, I felt the hands of the shadows, my pursuers, touching me on the shoulders. This time, however, it didn't worry me. I didn't turn round, as I was certain they would eventually show themselves to me of their own accord and that the moment of our meeting was not far off. That's what they were trying to tell me when they touched me; it was also an encouragement to take the next step that presented itself.

As soon as I opened the door I was assaulted by some sugary music, rather like supermarket muzak, and by a smell of the same kind, a whiff of baking, popcorn and cut flowers with the obligatory presence of certain artificial essences.

I entered a long corridor, lined with deserted toilets. Overlaying the synthetic music was a babble of laughter, whispers and sighs. I went a bit further and reached one of the wings of a huge auditorium, entirely decorated in sky-blue velvet drapes, with a vast pit separated into tiers, a whole host of boxes, dress circles, balconies and three overhanging galleries. From the orchestra pit to the gods, massed clouds of angels fluttered round and intertwined in great confusion.

Naked and beautiful, and for the most part bisexual, these creatures' sole activity seemed to be an uninterrupted pursuit of pleasure, in chairs which were often half broken and submerged in the clouds of feathers and down which fell from their wings and filled the whole room.

Yet the enormous stage, whose curtains had obviously been ripped down a long time ago, since there were still a few dirty, discoloured red shreds hanging, and whose boards were invisible beneath a thick layer of dust, was empty.

I walked slowly up the stalls, clearing a way through the first section. From all sides, angels brushed past me as they flew hither and thither, taking no heed of my presence, carried away with their incessant babbling, perpetually smiling, eternally youthful. They all had well-proportioned bodies, slim, slightly muscular, with supple, appetizing flesh and fine, entirely smooth skin. Many of them had the attributes of both sexes, magnificent, firm, round breasts together with a penis and testicles. Some of them were exclusively female or male, others were totally sexless, with a strangely smooth strip of flesh between their legs, others were hermaphrodite.

Some of the latter had female genitals above their male genitals, while others had them the other way round: their male cluster hanging over their female slit. They coupled in what struck me as the most perfect possible way: the upper cock of the first in the upper slit of the second and the lower cock of the second in the lower slit of the first. Each was simultaneously penetrator and penetrated, each was at the same time the man and woman of the other. And I imagined that they must experience the greatest ecstasy.

The other angels also embraced incessantly and without

any distinction of sex, stuck together, fluttering one to the other, from the stalls to the balcony and from the dress circle to the boxes, in total disorder, adopting every position imaginable for creatures free of the laws of gravity.

The pricks were constantly erect, the vulvas constantly swollen. The display of all these hairless genitals might easily have been obscene. But what struck me as particularly strange – for since I had entered the little circus I had noticed the place was detached from this particular obligation, unlike the outside world – was that all these sexes, including the female ones, were covered as far as the anus with a sophisticated form of condom, a very fine film of latex wrapped so tight over the skin it was almost as one with it. All these condoms were delicately tinted, in all the colours of the rainbow, as I soon noticed. 'If these creatures need protection,' I thought, 'perhaps the world I have found behind this door is, in spite of all appearances, closer to that which we normally call the real world . . .'

I noticed that, between the thick piles of feather and down, the floor was bestrewn with popcorn. I snacked on enough of this to placate my hunger, then I went to the back of the room where I found the stairs up to the upper galleries. I left all my clothes on a landing as I wanted to blend in with this mass of naked bodies, and I climbed up to the gods.

It was the same atmosphere up there as in the pit, perhaps even more confused, because of the relatively cramped spaces between the seats, and more fantastical, because of the pleasure the angels took in using the balcony rail for their unusual acrobatics.

I also had a high-up view of the stage, which stood deserted and abandoned in the middle of all this tumult and seemed even more desolate than ever. I noticed that none of the angels ever looked at it, as if they knew the sight of it would be too sad, almost unbearably so, and that it would spoil their pleasure.

I decided to imitate them and, turning my back on the stage, I mixed in among the throng and tried little by little to get involved in their games. I began by lavishing caresses on those around me, trying at first, in line with my tastes on the outside, to choose angels of the female type. But the sexes were so mixed up and there were too many of them. When I found myself kissing the buxom bosom of some creature who turned out to have a cock as big and erect as mine, I gave up trying to make these distinctions, which were entirely meaningless here.

I started touching everything that came my way and so I ended up, for the first time in my life, with a cock in my mouth, one belonging to a hermaphrodite angel who had stuck it in without asking as it flew level with my face. Because of its condom it had a slight aniseed taste and I was happy to keep it in my mouth as I admired and caressed the nice pussy opening up beneath its balls and which was also covered by a thin film of green latex. Almost immediately, a male angel came up behind it and penetrated its female sex as I was taking care of its other sex.

'We're spoiling you, aren't we, my pretty,' I thought. 'It won't be long before you come ...' And I began to wonder how, when they had come, they managed to remove and replace their condoms, which seemed stuck to their skin. But a moment later they both withdrew to fly away elsewhere, in different directions, without having achieved orgasm.

As for me, I was very excited. I got hold of a female angel who was standing next to me and penetrated her without waiting. It had big doe eyes and was the first really to look at me, with a truly angelic, charming smile. I caressed its long, silky blond hair and told myself that, despite my desire, I would be patient and give it enough time to take its pleasure from me.

That's when I noticed what I had missed in my haste. Once again I had ended up with a hermaphrodite. The feeling of its cock pushing its way between my buttocks left no doubt on that score. I was shocked and pulled away sharply. I immediately regretted being so brusque and wanted to apologize; but it was no use, for it had already flown away to new skies, still smiling and not the slightest bit bothered.

All these adventures had left me with a keen sense of frustration. 'You're not relaxed enough,' I told myself. 'Be like the others, let yourself go, and you will experience the same bliss.'

Around me it was turning into a party. The male and hermaphrodite angels were now taking each other in a line, one behind the other. The chain was already several dozen strong and was growing by the second. Without thinking, and with a burst of energy, I penetrated the open, pink arsehole stuck out in front of me. And then another angel came up behind me, since that was the law of the chain, and this time I went along with it. I felt the tip of its cock gently open my anus and then slide inside, finally penetrating me all the way. It started to give me a sweep, to the same rhythm as I dug into the one in front of me, the rhythm of the entire chain. The pain had given way to a strange joy, and I groaned, from both rage and pleasure, violence and submission, the desire to hurt and the desire to come.

Around us the female angels were making love with each other, or were having it done to them by the sexless angels, who were perhaps the keenest to fuck all the sexes, even if they only had their mouths and hands to do it with. Other angels, ones with cocks, left the chain to join in their games, and I promised myself I would do likewise, once I had finished with the males.

I noticed that, curiously, none of them had bothered to come before seeking new pleasures. Whereas I, since this was my first homosexual experience, intended to see, it through to the end, to experience the sensation of ejaculating in the firm behind of another male while feeling my own arse being invaded and pummelled by another dick. And I didn't take long. I let out a cry, my come shot out like an arrow.

Immediately, the angel I was buggering cried out too, separated from me and collapsed to the ground in tears. At the same time, the one who was in me pulled out sharply and in an instant the chain fell completely apart. There was an air of dejection throughout the whole gallery, which gradually turned into anger and delirium. Some angels pulled out their feathers, others clawed their breasts or spun round and round. Their faces slumped before my eyes, their bodies collapsed, their splendid flesh sagged, fattened and went horribly out of shape, lines appeared at the corners of their mouths and across their cheeks and foreheads ... Then they turned towards me, tried to intimidate me by spreading their wings, which creaked and crumbled pitifully and, all together, pointed their fingers at me.

'What's going on? What have I done?' I asked, flabbergasted.

'He came!' they cried in a tearful chorus.

'I don't understand ... Why shouldn't I have come?'

'He has blasphemed! Destroyed everything! We never come, you wretch, we have learned to forget about it! We forgot! That's why we are so beautiful! So pure! So perfect! Look what you've done to us!'

They grabbed hold of me, shook me violently, their eyes full of hate. I suddenly felt a strong sense of injustice and rebellion, and started to shout out myself:

'It's you who are wretched creatures! The sad audience of a void which you refuse to see! What are you doing in this theatre with no plays, imprisoned together, desiring each other but never able to come?'

But these words only made them more furious. Several of them even seemed to have gone mad. They covered their ears with both hands, screamed hysterically and shook their heads from left to right, as if to deny what I had done and said. Others became violent and came at me like a lynch mob. Fortunately my pleasure had caused them to lose a lot of their strength and I managed to get away.

I left the gods, collected my clothes from the landing and got dressed, and then left by the first exit I found at the foot of the stairs. I felt bruised and weak. Sad too, as if these deplorable creatures had managed to contaminate me with their taste for non-existence. I spat on the ground, to show what I thought of them.

I was in the middle of a crossroads of corridors.

DOOR 6.

DOOR 2.

2

The Dog

It was completely dark. I hesitated for a moment with my hand on the door, then my curiosity got the better of me and I entered.

I felt my way forward along the wall. There was a corner, leading in, then another, leading out, as if marking a change of room. Then I heard a metal grille descend and I found myself locked in a cell, behind bars.

I started calling out, without success. I made several tours of my meagre space, hoping to find a possible exit, and I shook the grille several times with all my strength, before I finally curled up on the ground and tried to sleep in order to banish my anxiety, caused by a feeling that time had been halted by my incarceration, by the silence and the dark.

In the end I got to sleep, but I was brutally woken up by a kick to my thigh. A harsh light was shining on me. I screwed up my eyes and saw, under the raised grille, a woman dressed in thigh-length boots and PVC underwear, who was holding a lead that was attached to a dog collar round my neck.

'Come out of your hole, you filthy beast,' she said.

And she gave a violent tug on the chain. I was about to

get up when I received another kick from the pointed toe of her boot.

'On all fours!' she ordered, in a tone which brooked no discussion.

I obeyed her. As I walked behind her I raised my eyes from her stiletto heels to her little bottom, which was barely covered by her very narrow pants and which minced nicely. She was slim and well built and very sexy in her tight, shiny synthetic-leather undies. Her corset, laced at the back, accentuated the curve of her hips.

I followed my mistress into the sitting-room. In one corner of the room a fat man in a silk dressing gown was lounging on the sofa and smoking a cigar.

'This filthy beast has been naughty again,' said the fat man, looking at me in an evil way. 'If this carries on we will have to tan his hide.'

'Don't worry, I'll put him in his place,' said the woman.

She led me to the kitchen. My knees were beginning to hurt. She put a big pile of mince in a bowl, went back to the lounge and placed it at the foot of the sofa.

'Eat,' she said.

And without letting go of my lead, she sat down next to the fat man, opened his dressing gown and started to wank him. I tentatively placed a hand on her thigh, hoping to be given permission to join in their games, but I received a kick in the ribs.

'You fat pig!' the woman shouted. 'Are you going to eat your meat?'

I bent over the bowl, took three small mouthfuls and swallowed them with some difficulty.

'That's better, good dog,' said my mistress, stroking the back of my neck. 'In return, you can lick me,' she added, offering me her foot.

I began to run my tongue from the pointed toe to the high heel. The fat man watched me, his eyes alight with lechery. The woman had just gone down on his little dick, which began to stiffen, and she started to suck it.

I continued to lick her boots assiduously. When I saw that they were both too wrapped up in their fornication to notice me, I undid my trousers and, while she was busy with her sucking, I rubbed myself off against her leg, like a real dog would do.

I came more quickly than the fat man. They hadn't noticed a thing. I slipped out of my collar and went discretely to the door, glancing back at my semen running down the vinyl boots. I felt like laughing.

I did up my flies in the corridor and opened the following door.

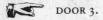 DOOR 3.

3

Jane and the Marsupilami

Everything was green. Everything except the turquoise stream and the red wood of the palm-roofed huts in the clearing. It was virgin forest, impenetrable, filled with the calls of humming birds and cockatoos.

I left the edge of the forest and headed towards the huts, which stood at the side of a path.

There were no more than a dozen of them, and there was no one to be seen, but there must be civilization here because two of them had signs over the door: the sign on the longer one said BAR, and on the shorter one, whose roof was equipped with a load of sophisticated antennae, the sign said BANK. They seemed to be in good nick, not abandoned.

I carried on as far as the stream, which I could see sparkling through the leaves, and I discovered that it was bordered on both banks by walls of stones, carefully placed on top of each other, about fifty centimetres high. I sat on top of the little wall and watched the shimmering stream. Then I saw a monstrous head rise up out of the water, which snorted noisily then began to emit guttural cries.

I leapt to my feet. But it was just a man, a local, his face half covered by an old diving mask, and he was celebrating.

He came out of the water, his arms raised in victory, laughing and dancing comically on his frail legs which emerged from his soaking, over-large shorts. The tanned skin of his chest was marked diagonally, from the left collar bone to the sternum, by the scar of what seemed to be a knife wound.

He came towards me, still hopping and delirious with joy, and opened his hands in front of my face. I recoiled a little, for the nearness of what he was holding made my eyes light up. In each palm he held a large, shiny nugget of gold.

'Gold, mate!' he said. 'Gold.'

And taking off his mask he pointed to the stone walls.

'See all that? I pulled all that out of the stream to see more clearly. Nice work, eh?'

He looked proudly at his work, thousands of stones patiently collected and piled up.

'Now there's nothing left but nuggets. I need only dive down and help myself. Here, mate!'

And he shoved a nugget into my hand.

'Take it! Take it! I'm giving it to you!'

He was delighted to see the surprise and incredulity on my face, delighted by his own generosity. His small hazel eyes shone.

'Hee-hee! Come on, the drinks are on me.'

He dragged me off to the bar. On the way I looked at the nugget. It was shaped like two buttocks, or a heart, depending on which way you looked at it. I wondered whether to keep it or sell it. It depended on how much it was worth. These days it's probably better to find a bank card than a gold nugget. I put it in my pocket.

The bar was dark and made entirely of wood; it looked like a saloon. As we came in the four drunkards leaning on the bar slowly turned their heads, as one man, towards us, without blinking; their bodies stayed totally still and relaxed. There was a sly-looking old man, a tall beanpole with a stupid smile and two ruddy-faced types, of average height but solidly built, who must have been in their early thirties and looked like brothers.

'The drinks are on me,' my goldminer repeated for the benefit of the barman, a tall chap with a handlebar moustache, who lined up six glasses of beer on the bar.

After this, everyone bought a round. In the ceiling a large fan stirred up the oppressive air as they recounted their latest goldmining adventures, or trotted out their old stories, which they all knew, and which were all about discovering ever more extraordinary seams and making and losing fortunes in a matter of days.

My 'friend' led them to believe that I had found a nugget right under his nose, just like that, by bending down, and he invited me to show it off to them, making out that he had never met anyone as lucky as me, and he seemed to derive some mysterious kudos from all this. The others looked at my treasure and shook their heads, clearly impressed. Since I had become some sort of hero, I offered to buy another round.

I must have knocked back a few pints, but it was just as hot. The conversation became more and more meandering and my shirt was sticking to my skin. I asked where the toilets were. I was shown a corridor at the end of the room.

There was no light other than the vague glimmer of the

sign marking the toilets at the end of the corridor. I went towards it, staggering a little because of the beer. When I tried to lean against the wall to guide myself, I found that, on both sides, my hands touched against bars.

At the same time I realized there was something alive behind these bars, for I could hear sounds of rubbing and breathing. My first thought was that I was in a narrow alley-way in a circus menagerie, between cages of monkeys and other wild animals. But my head was too befuddled to ponder this any further and my most urgent preoccupation was with finding the toilets, where I could throw up and piss out all the excess liquid that was swilling round my body like a choppy sea.

As I returned to the bar, I heard myself being called to on all sides, from the cages. The voices were whispering, but were unlike those of the shadows in the corridors, who always called me by my name, whereas these used the language of prostitutes: 'Looking for business, darling?' and other such things. Although I was still drunk, I got the message: in this village consisting solely of a few huts belonging to goldminers with primitive methods, there was none the less a bank, a small one, but still connected by modern systems of communications to the banking establishments and stock markets of the world, a bar with a plentiful supply of beer and other alcoholic drinks, and a brothel.

I leant against the bars of one cage to see if I could make anything out inside and the door opened of its own accord. At the back of the room, to the right, I saw a bed, on which lay the voluptuous form of a naked young woman with her back towards me.

'Come, oh, please, come quickly,' she whispered over and over again, her voice burning with desire.

I took off my clothes, dropped them on the ground and went to lie down next to her on the bed. She still lay obstinately with her back to me, but she had such ample hips and such a splendid bum that far from complaining about her position I grabbed her by the hips and stuck my cock between her buttocks. She slid it out and pushed it into her cunt, for she was so excited it seemed she was smeared with lubricant between her legs. She said not a word throughout.

She had soft skin, a supple body, she was amazingly docile and her vagina was so elastic it sucked and squeezed your dick with the combined talents of an expert mouth and hands. It took me a long time, because of the alcohol, and I felt the pleasure slowly rising within me and came in the girl's belly. I went straight to sleep, holding her in my arms and still inside her.

I didn't realize until I woke up: I had fucked an inflatable doll, her lascivious invitations had come from a tape recorder on the bedside table. Now that my eyes were used to the dark I turned it over and looked at it from all angles. She was bloody shapely, she had a nice pair of pointed breasts and a pretty face, with large eyes that seemed to be imploring you for something, and juicy lips opened just wide enough to take you in.

'So you lied to me, you dirty little whore,' I said.

And to punish her I stood above her, my legs apart, and pissed on her face. Then I grabbed her by the hair and stuck my dick in her mouth.

'So, bitch, what do you say to that?'

She didn't say a thing, but it felt as if she had a vacuum-cleaner nozzle between her lips. I held her by the hair and pulled her head backwards and forwards, her large eyes looked more and more surprised, and she sucked my gland like some highly efficient orgasm machine, while I took advantage of the situation to shower her with insults and obscenities. All this filth, which was my revenge for the treachery I had suffered, went to my head. I started to grip her throat between my hands, pressing with all my strength with my thumbs and, at the moment the latex exploded under the pressure, I ejaculated.

I crawled around the cage on all fours, looking for my clothes. But they had vanished. I found nothing except a sort of loincloth in imitation leopardskin, a ridiculous-looking thing which I put on anyway, for want of something better.

Apparently the bar was closed. There was no one about and the door was locked from the inside. I was almost relieved, for I wasn't keen to be seen in this garb. I looked outside through the window. No one there either. Apart from the little old man squatting on the ground in the shade. Perfect. I opened the door and went towards him.

As soon as he saw me he guffawed and slapped his thigh, then, pointing at me, started laughing like an idiot, punctuating it with high-pitched hiccups. I would have liked to punch his face to shut him up but he looked too frail.

'Where are my clothes?' I asked him in a sufficiently threatening tone of voice to make him reply.

Between hiccups he pointed to the top of a tree. As I approached the enormous trunk I saw that my clothes had 17 been placed on a large branch, neatly folded with my shoes on top. Luckily there was a solid-looking creeper hanging from this branch.

I started climbing, as if on a climbing rope. The branch was several metres above the ground. Each time I stretched to pull myself up, my sex, which was dangling free below the end of the cloth that was supposed to protect my modesty, rubbed gently against the vine. When I reached the top I had a hard-on and I was almost sorry the climb was over.

There was something strange about this tree. It was in fact a false tree, a prop tree. The wood, the bark, the leaves, the creepers were all imitation. I raised my eyes to the other trees in the jungle to see whether they were as false as mine. That's when I saw, sitting comfortably in the branches of a neighbouring tree, a superb creature of flesh and blood, a quite beautiful woman dressed only in a loincloth like mine. And indeed it was my loincloth she was staring at, licking her lips.

I too lowered my eyes to the object of her curiosity and greed and I saw that my cock, still erect because of the creeper and now even more so because of the sight of this naked pin-up, had lifted the edge of the cloth and its tip was sticking out.

I looked back at the girl, who was still interested in my manhood, so interested in fact that she started to fondle her breasts, then moved her hands over her stomach, her thighs, and then finally opened her legs wide, lifted her loincloth and caressed herself ardently, still staring at my cock, which was stiffer than ever.

I grabbed hold of a creeper and this time used it to swing

across to her, without taking my eyes off her. The sight of her there, panting, her head back in the leaves, together with the contact of the creeper, almost made me come in mid-air. But I managed to contain myself and reached her at the very moment she achieved orgasm. As she was coming, I stuck my cock against her stomach, which made it stand up even more. Then I penetrated her immediately, placing her magnificent legs around my neck.

My child of the wild had platinum-blonde hair, immaculately plaited and lacquered, eyes made up to seem slightly bigger, painted lips, entirely hairless legs, armpits and sex, twenty polished nails and skin imbued with some luxurious perfume. The white bikini marks showed the very narrow portions of her body which modesty prevented her from revealing on the beach. She started arching back again and crying out, and I forced myself to make the whole thing last as long as possible, for the show she put on as she took her pleasure was so intense that you wanted to see it start again straight away.

After a while I thought I'd seen enough of the front view and I turned her round and took her doggy fashion, from the flip side. She hung onto the branches and jerked her hips furiously, mewling and moaning, shaking her mane of hair every which way. It was all too much for me.

I was about to come with her when a hairy monster, yellow with black spots, seemed to fall from the sky and ripped her away from me. Before I knew what was going on she had grabbed hold of him with a cry of joy and, with a few leaps, he had carried her away to the top of the neighbouring tree.

I found myself alone in less time than it takes to say it, my sex erect in mid-air and sorely abandoned. Over yonder, my Jane was trembling with joy and playing with the tail of the Marsupilami, for indeed it was he (I had recognized his victory cry, that distinctive 'houba, houba' with which he taunted me). It seemed I was out of the running. With his tail he could satisfy her in all sorts of unbeatable ways, like, for example, tying her up and penetrating her at the same time. And she had an even better orgasm.

So I made do with playing the voyeur. I ended up sitting astride a branch watching them. My sperm spurted out like a fountain and fell from branch to branch, from leaf to leaf, to the ground, where it would fertilize the earth. I went back to my branch, lost the loincloth, put my clothes on and climbed back down the creeper. When I reached the bottom I remembered to look for the nugget in my pocket. It was still there. And how beautiful it was! I turned it over lovingly between my fingers. I looked across to the huts and, through the foliage, tried to make out the banks of the stream. I should go and bid farewell to the man who had shown me such generosity, even if I hadn't the slightest desire to see the others.

I was walking towards the river with my hands in my pockets and the nugget in the hollow of my hand, when I felt the nugget soften and go out of shape in the warmth of my palm. I could barely bring myself to look at it. When I opened my hand it was smeared with brown stains, by a dark-brown paste seeping out through the tears in the gold paper.

I threw the chocolate nugget to the ground, in the synthetic grass, licked my palm clean and returned to the place where I had come in, the door at the back of the scenery which returned me to the dark corridors, where two doors offered themselves to me.

☞ DOOR 4,

☞ DOOR 5.

4

The Player

'Hurry, hurry, Miss Mariella is waiting for you!'

The man dragged me through the changing rooms to the treatment room. Lying on the massage table, a tennis player in a white skirt welcomed me with a smile.

'You're Paul's replacement?' she said as she held out her hand. 'I presume he's explained it to you. He always massages my calves and thighs before I go out on court.'

'Of course,' I said, returning her smile.

She had magnificent legs, long, lean and muscular, and if she took me for the replacement for her physio, then I had to play the role and not disappoint her. If I tried hard enough I'd soon find a suitable way to warm up her precious muscles.

Miss Mariella closed her eyes and waited for me to set to work. I approached the table. In that position she looked like some delicacy laid out for my delectation. I grabbed her left leg, pulled it away from her right. Her skin was elastic, smooth and tanned. I bent her knee and started to massage her calf, running my fingers the whole length of her firm, supple flesh.

A half-smile of relaxation spread across her face. She was so feminine and ravishing, with her fine, chestnut hair pulled back and gathered in a coloured tie, a few short curls hanging loose, with her oval face, her high cheekbones, her little nose, her discreet make-up, her air of determination mixed with an impression of freshness and gaiety.

I moved up to her fine, round knee. Under her white top her plump little breasts rose gently with each breath. At the hem of her pleated skirt I could see where her knickers fastened between her legs with three press studs. I spent a long time massaging her thighs, moving as far up as my role permitted. I had an erection.

Then she got up and told me to keep an eye on her during the match, in case she needed my services. I crossed my fingers to wish her good luck and went out into the stand as she emerged on court.

The crowd raised the roof as she stepped out. Her opponent was there too, a tall blonde, severe-looking, slim and well-built. Throughout the whole match she played a stream of hard strokes to the back of the court, while Mariella, lively and mobile, continually came up to the net and covered the whole clay court as if she were performing figures in a ballet, as if she were fulfilling the rites of some cosmic ceremony which consisted of glorifying every inch of a demarcated space.

I was sitting in the front row. When she was playing at the far end, I could see the killer look in Mariella's eyes when she served, a look designed to weaken the unwavering psychological strength and the solid physical and technical qualities of her opponent. And when she was at this end I could better admire the play of her legs and her knickers.

Her knickers, which she revealed completely when she 23

was waiting for her opponent to serve, bouncing on the spot and swinging her racquet from left to right, or every time that her skirt flew up when she raised her arms and threw her body forward to make a serve or a smash.

Twice, during breaks, she called me over to give her right thigh a quick massage, where she had felt a slight tightening of the muscle. But the match was very close and I felt that she didn't even see me, didn't see anything of the outside world, so focussed was she in herself. Finally she won the match in three sets, 7–6, 6–7, 8–6.

She greeted her victory with a raised fist. All the time she was out on court she was radiant, as if filled by the applause raining down on her. But as soon as she returned to the dressing room I could see that she was extremely serious and, far from being relieved after the tension of the match, she seemed even more wrapped up in herself and her anxiety.

She dragged me into the treatment room. She opened a metal locker and, standing on tiptoe to reach the top shelf, took out a riding crop, which she handed to me. Then she crouched down on the massage table, undid the studs on her knickers, pulled the two halves up over her waist, and, offering me her gorgeous, naked bottom, which was whiter than her tanned thighs, she said: 'Let's go.'

I mumbled something, incredulous, unable to believe what she wanted me to do. She turned towards me with a blank expression and repeated: 'Let's go.'

Her plump little bottom was sticking out in front of me. It was as if it were looking at me. I raised the crop and
whipped it gently.

When the lash touched her flesh she gave a jerk. The blow left a light mark on her skin, which started to turn pink. I hesitated a moment. But she arched her back even more to incite me to continue. I struck her again, several times in a row.

I continued cautiously, so as not to hurt her too much. Her buttocks were now covered in bright red stripes, but she still wanted more. Her backside jerked under each blow, but otherwise she didn't flinch.

However, she finally let out a moan of pain. Then, I don't know why, I had a taste of blood in my mouth, and I started wielding the crop with all my strength. The lash descended, she gave a cry, a trace of red appeared on her buttocks.

I was breathing hard, it was hypnotic. I raised my arm again and hit her again and again and again, getting more and more excited as she moaned and cried at the violence of the blows, as the shiny red tears seeped through each break in her skin. Finally I got onto the table with her and, kneeling behind her, with my trousers down, I roughly penetrated her bruised arse and fucked her. She screamed, twisted, choked hysterically and I had to hold her by the hair as I thrust my hips into her. Then she started sobbing. I came as I had beaten her, with a sort of savagery.

'Thank you,' she said as she got up.

She wiped away her tears, much calmer now, and passed a white towel over her bottom, which became stained with red. I was beginning to regret what had happened, all the more as I hadn't seen her achieve her pleasure.

'But you didn't come,' I said.

'That's not what I look for in pain,' she replied. 'Pain doesn't give me any pleasure.'

'Then why . . . ?'

'Because I need this pain to distract me from another sort of pain, much more terrifying – I don't know what to call it or where it comes from, but when it appears, it threatens to become unbearable. In a way, I choose to suffer so as not to die of a greater suffering.'

'This unbearable pain, why not try to forget it through pleasure instead?'

'I love pleasure too much to spoil it in this way. I take my pleasure when I feel good. That's when it's best . . .'

As I left the room she gave me a little farewell wave and said:

'Do you think we might understand something about life one day?'

And she headed off into the showers.

So as not to follow her I washed myself in the sink and wondered whether I had really lost control or whether this feeling of being out of control wasn't just a trick invented by my mind to free me of the weight of what I had done.

I went back out into the dark corridors, where I wandered for a long time before I opened a door.

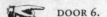 DOOR 6.

5

The Collection

I found myself in a lift. I would probably have stepped straight out if it hadn't been occupied by a young girl who greeted me with a smile. She pressed a button and we started to go up.

We were standing in opposite corners, facing each other. She was simply dressed in jeans, boots and a jacket. She had a large photographer's portfolio at her feet and was carrying a square 6 × 6 camera round her neck. She was checking me over from head to foot with a frank, direct gaze.

'Do you want me to turn round?' I joked.

'I want to show you something,' she said.

She bent down, took a file out of her portfolio and came over to me. The file contained a collection of pornographic photos, bodies and sexes of men and women, couples in action.

'Did you take these?' I asked.

'I have several clients ... Collectors ... They pay well.'

'Good for you.'

'Would you like to pose for me?'

'For a rich female collector?'

'Yes. Here in the lift will be fine. Open your shirt, drop   27 your trousers, that's all ... Thanks, that's great. Oh! I'm sure they will adore ...'

She measured the light down between my legs and took a first series of snaps in close-up. She made me strike different poses and encouraged me:

'Very good ... Yes, like that ... Very nice ...'

Then she knelt at my feet and started to suck me. I thought the shoot had turned her on, but I realized she only wanted me to get an erection for the rest of her reportage. As soon as I was stiff, she started shooting off film.

She photographed me from every angle, with my dick erect, then she asked me to pretend to be wanking. Finally she had the good grace to finish sucking me off. But my contribution was not yet at an end. When she felt that I was on the point of coming, she placed my cock back in my hand and picked up her camera. I ejaculated right onto her lens.

When I left her she blew me a little kiss. The doors closed and the lift whisked her away.

I walked in the corridor for a while, trying to imagine what effect my photos would have on the rich collectors who would buy them. What would they do with them exactly? I hoped there was at least one pretty woman among these sluts ... A pretty woman who would dream about me as I was dreaming about her ...

Then I stopped thinking about it and opened a door.

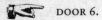 DOOR 6.

6

The Exchange

I entered a rustic house, a barn made of roughly hewn stones cemented with earth. In a corner of the large single room a log was burning slowly in the fireplace. Opposite, there was a pile of wood stacked against the rough white wall, the only wall where the stone had been covered and along which there were several shelves of books.

The room was a mixture of roughness and comfort, with a concrete floor tinted pink, a colourful carpet whose white background showed the dust, a sofa in black fabric with a small white motif, two rattan chairs painted white, two armchairs in blue fabric and, in the kitchen, all the latest electrical goods, a large trestle table and two rough wood benches.

Three Chinese lampshades in red paper, which hung down between the beams of the low roof, made the place look a bit like a gambling den, while the bathroom door, which still hadn't been painted and had no latch, contributed to the unfinished feel of the whole thing. In the centre of the room a large square opening in the ceiling revealed the loft, which was reached by a ladder. There was a wooden rail running around this hole and I was expecting to see a brace of girls in petticoats leaning over it, smiling at me. I placed myself in the centre, right beneath them, perfectly placed to make my choice. But no one came.

I stood in front of a large mirror with a dark red frame and checked how I looked, as if I were waiting for an important meeting, and then I climbed up.

The loft was divided into three levels, which marked out three small bedrooms or sleeping quarters. One of these was separated from the others by various bits of cloth hanging from the beams. I pulled them apart and went inside the end room.

It was almost entirely taken up by a large bed with metal posts facing a French window which framed a magnificent, luminous mountain landscape, entirely white with snow. In the bed a woman reclined on a couple of large pillows. She had a cardboard folder resting on her lap, on which lay a white sheet of paper which she was covering with blue ink.

'Hello,' she said. Indicating the bed, she continued, 'Please sit down. If you just give me a couple of minutes ... I just have to finish a little description then I'm all yours ...'

And she continued writing.

Behind the bed two sets of shelves full of books formed a sort of partition on each side of the two red curtains which marked the entrance to the room. It was the same theatrical dark red as the frame of the large mirror on the ground floor, and it appeared here also on another large oval mirror and on the bed spread. Leaning against the lowest part of the roof there was also a board on which were pinned a number of postcards and photos, among which I recognized pictures of Kafka, Poe, Céline in his garden, Rimbaud,

Verlaine sitting in a bistro in front of a glass of absinthe,

Baudelaire, Tolstoy with his beggar's stick ... And a reproduction of *Philosophy Meditating* by Rembrandt, another of an engraving representing a ruined Roman church in a landscape of sand and pines ... And photos ... A small boy reading on a beach, his chin resting on his knee, a plump, naked baby sitting in a chair sucking its thumb, a young woman in shorts sleeping on a park bench – the same woman who was lying on the bed writing – a young man in a hat and dark glasses lying full-length on a road, the same man reading on a hotel bed with a full moon shining in the night sky through the window ...

I turned to look at the mountain.

'Do you see that summit over there with the tall aerial? It's the Pic du Midi,' she said, without stopping writing. 'That's where they take the best photos of the sun's corona. And at night they observe the sky ... It's beautiful, isn't it?'

She seemed to be lost in wonder. I agreed politely, wondering what she was driving at. She didn't say any more. I reached out my hand to touch her leg through the covers. But she pulled it away, apparently amused by this. She was still absorbed in her writing.

'Haven't you finished your description yet?' I said, slightly annoyed.

'Yes, just done. Now we'll be able to talk.'

But she carried on writing. I leaned over her piece of paper and I saw that she had just noted down the exact question I had just asked her and the reply she had given. And at this precise moment she was recounting that I was reading her piece of paper.

'What do you think you're doing?' I asked.

This time she looked me in the eye, still scribbling away. Her eyes were dark, shiny and wide open, making her look almost stupid or as if she were hallucinating.

'I'll explain,' she said. 'Let's not be formal. It is I who am writing your adventures.'

'You're a reporter?'

'Not exactly. To be a reporter I'd have to follow you ...'

'Ah, I get it. You're the one who's been following me in the corridors?'

'No, not me. I stay here, in my bed. To tell you the truth, I invented all this, the kingdom of Eros, the doors, the shadows who follow you in the corridors, the adventures, the characters, the Woman ... and you, of course.'

'I see. If I understand you correctly, I only exist in your imagination.'

'Of course not, not solely. Here, touch yourself. You see you are made of flesh and blood. Particularly flesh – I hope you have had plenty of opportunity to verify that since you have been in here ...'

'How can I be in your head and in my body at the same time?'

'I don't know. I am in your head, too, and still in my own body. You see, at this precise moment you are inventing me as much as I am inventing you ...'

I was silent for a moment, then I continued:

'If everything is written ... that means I am not the master of my own actions nor of my own destiny ...'

'Nothing is written in advance. Everything is written as we experience it. It is simply a matter of how we perceive time. Do we ever know where the present is? In the past, in the future, it is everywhere and nowhere ...'

'Perhaps ... All that's very well, but there's one thing I don't agree with. You see everything I do, you even see me in the most private situations, but I can't see anything of you. So why don't we talk about you for a bit? For example, to turn things round a bit, what turns you on?'

'You're being really unfair. Or you're blind. I'm constantly exposing myself. You see as much of me as I see of you: all these corridors you walk down are in my mind, all these doors you open are inside me. You see, we have millions of doors in there,' she continued, tapping her head. 'There are people who, their whole life long, open only a few of these doors, while you and I transform this labyrinth into the most thrilling area of adventure and exploration. Each time you open a door, you open it both in my head and in yours. So you know as much about me as I know about you ...'

'Ye-e-es ... But all the same, you make me do what you want, yet it doesn't work the other way round.'

'Do you believe that? You should have heard me when I had enough of your erotic frenzy. I admit that on those occasions I slagged you off in the most inelegant terms. Sometimes I had it up to here with your insatiable sexual appetites. But I carried out my task ... For you ...'

'I can see now why you made me do some bizarre things ... And now, may I know what is going to happen to me? Will I find the Woman?'

'That all depends on you. On the way you deal with the final tests. But first the time has come to meet the shadows.'

'And ... what about you and me?' I added knowingly, leaning towards her.

'You and I are everything. That's enough, isn't it?'

She got up, climbed down the ladder, opened the door of the barn and went out into the corridor with me.

This time they were there. Two motionless silhouettes in the dark, one wrapped in a dark red cloth, the other in a black cloth. My heart started pounding against my chest.

'Meet the Shadow of Lost Love,' my companion said.

The red shadow came towards me, took me by the hand and said in a warm, affecting voice: 'Come.'

'And here is the Shadow of Yourself.'

The black shadow advanced, took my other hand and said in a serious, penetrating voice: 'Come.'

At the end of the corridor an illuminated sign indicated the exit. I realized I had reached the end of my journey. There were only two doors left, but I could just as easily give them a miss.

I turned to my companion, who was leaving me already.

'And the Woman?' I asked.

'Outside,' she said. 'You will find her outside.'

Terror and desire were battling it out in my veins. Now, no doubt, I was not far away from the great moment. Everything would depend on the choice I would make between:

– following the Shadow of Lost Love:

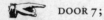 DOOR 7;

– or not:

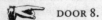 DOOR 8.

34

7

The Shadow of Lost Love

'Who are you?' I asked the Shadow of Lost Love.

In the dark I could only make out the dark red shape and the white glimmer of her long hair. She lowered her head and her face was hidden in the darkness.

'Come, please . . .' she moaned.

Suddenly I recalled a memory from my childhood. Our dog had disappeared. Despite searching all over we didn't find her until a week later. She had been discovered by a hunter at the bottom of a dry well in the forest. When we returned to the spot with him, bringing ropes to get her out, we heard a soft whining. That timid lament expressed all her exhaustion, but also her love and faithfulness. Lying at the edge of the hole, the child that I was hid his face in his hands and started crying with the dog, out of compassion and fear of emptiness.

And now it was as if the Shadow of Lost Love had fallen down a well and was waiting for me to save her.

She ushered me through a padded door into a small, circular pink room. The bed, which was also round, stood in the centre of the room. It was the only piece of furniture, but it still almost filled this confined space. The vaulted ceiling cast a weak, opalescent light over everything.

The Shadow had turned her back and moved ahead of me. Her strange, magnificent white hair fell down to her waist, making a striking contrast with the scarlet cloth wrapped around her like an ancient tunic.

'You see how my hair has turned white since I've been waiting for you, my love?' she said. 'But you are here at last and once again, and more than ever, we will be united in the most burning passion . . . See, I am yours.'

She moved her right hand over her left shoulder, the cloth fell, she was naked.

She was so beautiful she made me breathless. She was like a statue. Venus rising from the waves, seen from behind. I approached her and placed my hands on her hips, which seemed to have been sculpted by a god.

'You are beautiful,' I said.

Was it her beauty that so moved me? Or did she seem so beautiful because of the emotion which emanated from her? When I asked her to turn to face me, she refused.

'You mustn't see me,' she said.

'But why?'

'I don't want you to see me. I beg you . . .'

I was taken aback.

'Get undressed,' she whispered.

'Look, this is stupid.'

'Please . . .'

I took off my clothes. Then I picked up my shirt, ripped a strip off it and tied it round my eyes.

'I can't see you any more,' I said, placing my hand gently
on her shoulder.

She turned round and gave me a long kiss on my mouth, pressing her body against mine.

I pulled her onto the bed, which was just behind us. We continued to exchange kisses and caresses. I felt feverish and clumsy, no doubt because of the emotion which had taken hold of me since I had followed this woman and because she had forbidden me to look at her. Even though her body was superb to touch, I couldn't get an erection.

She moved down my body and took my sex in her mouth. But, despite all her efforts, nothing happened. I felt more and more uncomfortable. To take her mind off my discomfiture and to gain a little time I moved down between her legs and kept my face pressed in there for as long as possible. She held me by the neck, raised her hips, doing her best to achieve her pleasure. But it soon became obvious it wasn't working for her either.

Suddenly I could no longer tolerate this blindfold over my eyes. I ripped it off angrily. And I saw her.

Naked, lying on her back in the middle of the round bed, her alabaster body was as I had touched it, perfectly proportioned. Her long hair lay loose around her face and shoulders like a soft halo of light. She had the features of a madonna, overwhelming in their grace and humility. Her lips were tender and pink, like the nipples of her small, round breasts. Her waist curved harmoniously, her stomach was firm, her navel fresh and pretty as a heart, her silky mound as white and fascinating as her hair, her thighs plump, her calves smooth, her feet slender, her ankles fine, her hands delicate, her arms soft and gentle, her shoulders voluptuous, her neck elegant, her earlobes subtly outlined and joined directly onto her delicious face ... everything about this woman was ravishing, everything was perfect. Except her eyes. Her glassy, turned-up eyes had no life in them.

I probably observed her for quite a while, motionless, kneeling before her body. Suddenly she realized what was going on. She sat up straight and felt for my face. I didn't hide away. When she verified that I had taken off my blindfold, she lay down on her stomach and started crying, her head on her arms.

'Don't cry ... Please don't cry ...' I said, caressing her slowly.

She was more beautiful than ever. I felt a surge of desire. My cock was so erect it almost hurt me. But I wanted to be nice to her. I gently coaxed her to turn over. Tears flowed copiously from her white globes and soaked her cheeks, her hair, her throat, right down to her bosom. I finally got her onto her back and penetrated her.

She let out a deep sigh and then continued crying her eyes out, with moans both of pleasure and pain. I leant over her to kiss her wet lips, her wet neck, her wet breasts, then I looked at my cock, which she couldn't see, moving all the way in and out between her thighs, which I held wide open; and again tasted the salty liquid coming out of her turned-up eyes like a slow, plaintive, delicious orgasm and I asked her not to cry, even though her tears were bringing me to the pitch of excitement.

At the last moment I pulled out of her to ejaculate over her blind, already damp face. The sperm came out in large spurts and formed into heavy blobs at the sides of her mouth, on her cheeks and at the corners of her white eyes.

I tenderly wiped her face with the strip I had torn from my shirt.

'Oh, my love,' she said, 'I don't ever want to be separated from you again.'

'Me neither,' I said, taking her in my arms.

She was the woman I had always loved.

'Will you leave me?' she whispered.

'Why do you say that? I love you, I want to stay with you.'

'But I can't leave here. They won't let me leave, I know they won't.'

'Don't worry. I'm here. I'll take you with me. Trust me.'

'Oh, if only we had never left each other ... Do you see what the sorrow has done to me? My hair has turned white, I've lost my sight ...'

'But you are even more beautiful ... And I too have been unhappy ... So unhappy ...'

I held her more tightly in my arms and started crying softly, like her.

I couldn't say how, but these tears flowing out liberated me. I penetrated her again and we made love, embracing tightly. At the moment when I came I felt as if my sex was joining our tears, crowning and exalting their sweet sharpness.

She rested her head on my shoulder and went to sleep. I lay there pensive, staring at the walls and the vaulted ceiling. It seemed as if the room had closed in on the bed. The room was becoming smaller and smaller, more and more oppressive; my mind became confused; sometimes I recalled a specific memory of my former lovemaking with this woman lying at my side; other times I had a strong feeling of deceit and unreality.

'My love,' I whispered, 'I will never leave you again, never ...'

Yes, that's probably what I wanted. Wasn't this an extraordinary opportunity to kiss and to love forever my Lost Love, the love most people regret their whole life long?

I got up, taking care not to wake her, and went out into the corridor.

Then I saw coming towards me, still dressed in black, the Shadow of Myself. The door of her room was still open behind her and I could see her bed, in the shape of a boat.

'Here,' she said, offering me a pebble. 'Keep this with you.'

I bent over to see it. It was a beautiful polished stone. I put it in my pocket.

Now it was time for me to leave. But a nagging anxiety prevented me from leaving alone. The feeling that there was no going back pierced me in the chest, and I tried to banish it by giving myself a choice. Confronted by the final exit, whose green light I could see not far ahead, at the end of the corridor, I convinced myself that I was still free, since I could still:

– go back and find the Shadow of Lost Love and bring her with me as I had promised her:

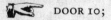 DOOR 10;

– or take the hand of the Shadow of Myself, to whom I felt irresistibly attracted, and take her with me to the exit:

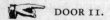 DOOR 11.

8

The Monster

The two shadows waited, squeezing my hands.

'I'm sorry,' I said. 'You are certainly very charming and I admit I am attracted and touched by your invitation. But it is time for me to bring an end to my wanderings in this labyrinth. Outside there is a real woman waiting for me and I don't want to compromise my chances of finding her.'

And, letting go of their hands, I headed for the exit.

At the end of the corridor, the illuminated sign called to me like a hope, a deliverance, an adventure. Would this last one be a happy one? There was a stab of apprehension in my desire to breathe the air of the outside world. Inside this dark kingdom, even if the journey had not always been easy, I had been exposed to some strange encounters and singular pleasures. Would I find so much emotion in the light of day? Would I be able to develop with the same mixture of anxiety and desire, with the same playful spirit? Wouldn't I simply succumb to the repetitive banality of everyday life, the tyranny of necessity? Would I be able to avoid the traps this world holds in store for that unfortunate creature we call human, the feeling of absurdity, the temptation of blindness, the submission to fate, boredom, renunciation, fear? Would I be able to love this woman who was waiting for me?

Before I reached the end of the corridor, I turned round. I saw the shadows, half submerged in the dark. They were embracing each other. It seemed as if they were exchanging a lovers' kiss. Then they disappeared behind one of the doors.

They had followed me in secret during my whole journey and I was throwing up the one opportunity I would ever have to see their faces uncovered. I turned round and went quickly back to the spot where I had seen them disappear. The door was still open.

I slipped quietly through the gap and found myself in a huge, square-shaped room, entirely covered by a mosaic, as in an ancient palace. The two shadows were there, naked. I recognized the Shadow of Lost Love by her long white hair. She was a gorgeous girl, like a living sculpture, an aesthetic masterpiece full of grace and softness, the very incarnation of a profoundly human ideal.

The Shadow of Myself was a more mature woman, but still beautiful and just as fascinating, with her dark, intelligent, extraordinarily lively gaze and her dominatrix appearance. She was perching on laced-up, high-heel boots, which were tightly moulded around her fine calves, and was wearing a glittering diamond crown in her black hair, which was cut short and square like an ancient Egyptian's. Otherwise, she was as naked as her companion. The cloths they had been wearing in the corridor, one purple and the other black, lay on the floor.

They hadn't heard me come in and I stood there in the doorway, not daring to disturb them. They both possessed a strange charm, which almost held me entranced. The pubic hair of the Shadow of Lost Love was the same silky white as the hair on her head. I never tired of looking at her body, her curves, her voluptuous hips, her round, pearly breasts ... And I was not the only one who had succumbed to her beauty: the Shadow of Myself had fallen at her feet, which she was kissing fervently.

The white shadow began to moan and for the first time I realized that her eyes were turned up, unless they had no pupils, for there was nothing between her lids but two white globes. How had I not noticed this before? It was as if this sightless beauty had the power to divest you too of your own sight.

This discovery almost made me sick, and yet I realized that it served only to increase the fascination of this woman. For although I had been greatly admiring her naked body, although I had also been deriving much pleasure from observing her companion's body, although I had seen them indulging in lovers' foreplay, it was only at the moment when I saw this empty gaze that I got an erection.

At the same moment, the Shadow of Myself turned towards me and gave me a knowing smile, signalling to me not to make a sound. Then she took the white shadow in her arms and, with an ease and strength that astonished me, carried her to the bed, which was shaped like a boat. She then carried over a chair from the corner of the room where she signalled me to sit, still without making a sound.

The Shadow of Lost Love lay motionless in the boat in the position in which she had been laid, on her back with her legs open. When I reached them, the black shadow came to me, undid my belt and my flies and let my trousers fall around my feet. I wanted to embrace her, but she prevented me.

'It's too late,' she said. 'You didn't want to follow us when the time was right ... Now you can do nothing but regret us ...'

'Is he there?' the white shadow cried out, sitting upright with a haggard look. And she started crying and mumbling: 'Oh, why did you leave, why did you leave?'

This time I reached out my hand to her, but again the black shadow stopped me.

'Don't do that,' she said. 'Believe me, you must not do that. I have another task for you, the destiny of all three of us depends on it. Please, listen to me and stay there, for we will have need of you soon. For now, enjoy the only pleasure we can give you.'

She sat me down gently in the chair, took my right hand and closed it round my cock. She had been so persuasive, had seemed so superior in her knowledge of the mysteries of life that I started to desire her even more ardently than her young companion. However, I trusted her completely and was ready to submit to her orders, even if I was prevented from touching either of them.

She joined her companion on the bed and set about consoling her. Large tears flowed incessantly from her white eyes, drenching her face and neck, trickled down to her nipples, making them stand up. She took her in her arms, opened her mouth with her tongue and gave her a long kiss as she caressed her breasts, her stomach, between her thighs, until the tearful beauty opened her legs to offer her pussy to the expert fingers that were massaging it.

Then the Shadow of Myself got up and took a little plastic pot out of one of the black cupboards that stood against the walls of mosaic. Then she made the white shadow crouch on top of the bed, held the pot between her open thighs and said with authority:

'Stop crying and piss.'

The girl complied immediately. I watched the stream splash down from between her intimate lips and I had to lessen the pressure of my hand on my cock so as not to come.

The black shadow placed the pot at the foot of the bed and pushed her face into her warm pussy and started licking and titillating her clitoris, then the whole vulva. Her young friend moaned, panted and arched her magnificent back with the pleasure of it. Finally she penetrated her with her tongue while rubbing her pink button with her thumb. Then she seemed to be possessed and arched back violently when she came, with guttural groans.

When they swapped roles, when the white shadow slid her face into her friend's intimate parts, I forgot the order I had been given. I was starting to get tired of being a spectator of their women's games. The white shadow was lapping away assiduously, on all fours between her mistress's thighs, sticking out her tongue regularly and artlessly, like a cat before a bowl of milk, while her delicious behind bounced up and down in the air, as if it were held by some invisible phantom. She was obviously missing something, something that only I in this room could give her.

Who could have resisted the sight of this sublime rump, this adorable bum so in need of love? I climbed onto the bed, placed myself behind her and penetrated her. They both cried out, no doubt through a mixture of surprise, anger and pleasure, and I came deep inside the belly of my beautiful Lost Love.

They chased me off the bed, still screaming and gesticulating more than ever, in a state of terror, as if they were expecting some terrible consequence of my disobedience. The white shadow in particular seemed to be completely demented. She began clawing at her face and body until it bled. I helped the black shadow prevent her hurting herself further. I took off my shirt and ripped off a strip with which I tied her wrists to the prow of the boat.

She was lying on her back and she gradually calmed down. That's when I noticed how pale she was. Her skin had become transparent and there were large blue veins standing out all over her face and body. At the same time her stomach began to swell alarmingly. I looked at the Shadow of Myself, seeking help, some explanation. But she was merely crying and trembling silently, stroking her friend's brow.

As she was now, if anything, too calm, I wanted to untie her hands. But she started writhing again, supporting herself on her feet, with her legs apart. Her face, however, showed no pain, or anything at all. It was as if what was happening to her were totally foreign to her. In truth, it was as if she were dead and something were seeking to get out of her.

'It's now that we need you,' said the Shadow of Myself.

And the tone of her voice surprised me. She opened one of her black cupboards and handed me a large kitchen knife.

Sometimes I can't seem to remember very well what really

happened then. Other times, even when I think I've forgotten everything, the images return with a hallucinatory clarity. At those moments I feel that my whole life consists solely in walking a wire, or a network of wires, in a sort of trance which allows me to forget the constant risk of falling and the efforts I have to make at each instant to preserve such a fragile balance.

A huge black cockroach was extracting itself from the belly of the Shadow of Lost Love. At the same time she was losing all her blood, which was flowing out of her sex in long, shining streams. I held the knife in my hand and was unable to move.

Now the monster had managed to get out from between the thighs of the white shadow and it raised its eyes to me, surprising, large, sad eyes which seemed to be asking for mercy.

'It's a female,' said the Shadow of Myself, 'her belly is full of vermin. Kill her, before she has time to lay. Kill her, or they will spread everywhere!'

The creature was still looking at me with its strangely human eyes. I went up to the bed, sank my blade into its shell, just behind the head, pulled it out, sank it in again, over and over, with all my strength. It writhed clumsily on its thin legs, while a thick white liquid oozed out of each of its wounds. The thought came to me that it was my sperm, and I felt despoiled and betrayed. I continued to strike it to make it give back everything it had taken from me which I hadn't wanted to give. The creature fell on its back on the ground, wiggled its foul legs a little, then ceased to move.

'It's over,' said the Shadow of Myself as she stayed my arm.

She took the knife and slit the monster's belly. Inside, thousands of tiny cockroaches swarmed feebly, in their death throes.

The black shadow looked at me, then turned away to vomit. Bent double, she retched violently and ejected a stone, which she caught in her hand. On the bed, the white shadow was dead. I slumped to the ground, put my head in my hands and started to cry.

'It was necessary,' said the black shadow, placing her hand on my hair.

I lay prostrate for a long time, as if hoping that the passage of empty time would wipe away everything that had happened.

'Get up now,' the shadow finally said. 'Come and help me.'

The mosaic floor was made up of trapdoors, which opened onto tombs.

'So you live over a cemetery,' I said to the shadow, somewhat disgusted.

She looked at me as if I were stupid and said simply:

'Obviously.'

We buried the two bodies and cried together over Lost Love, over that white shadow we had both loved, who was so beautiful and for whom we now had to grieve. Then I helped her to clean the room.

When the time came to part, the Shadow of Myself gave me the pebble she had thrown up. It was a beautiful polished stone.

'Keep it,' she said. Then she added: 'From now on you and I will be allied forever.'

I gave her a long kiss. We made love, we cried again and we went to sleep in each other's arms.

Then I put the pebble in my pocket and left her. I knew we would remain close whatever happened and that I could count on her, as she could count on me.

As I headed for the exit I told myself that once I was outside I could still choose between:

– leaving with the Woman I was about to meet:

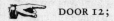 DOOR 12;

– or leaving alone:

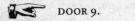 DOOR 9.

9

The Hermit

This afternoon Emilie came to see me. She had bought a mountain bike. She was flushed and out of breath when she arrived, but was very happy with her new toy, which she had proudly described to me in full detail. She said she could come and see me more often now. It was a long way on foot.

As it was a nice day I had put the table outside the cave to draw on. She took some cherries and some tobacco (for me) out of her rucksack. I made some tea and we sat out in the sun to have a chat.

She wanted to speak about Alaska again, but this time she had brought a little notebook to take some notes. She said that she would go there one day, to the same place I had been. She said that one day she would go everywhere I had been and write my life story. I know what she meant by 'one day': she meant when I was dead. I didn't say that to her because it would have upset her. But we both know that I am an old man and my days are numbered.

Emilie is the only one who doesn't try to convince me to come down to the village. They all think that, if I continue to live far away from people and doctors, I will die up here, alone, on the mountain. I'll die where I want to die.

Emilie went quite red when she told me about this book

she wanted to write about me. I could see it was her way of declaring her love for me. Then she asked if I would authorize her to do it and if I would help her by recounting everything. This time it was her way of asking if I recognized this love.

Well, I didn't answer straight away. Wouldn't she be better off having fun with people of her own age, rather than wearing herself out climbing up here to see me?

'Just for the book,' she added, as if she could read my thoughts. 'Please, it's very important to me ...

I said yes.

*

My name is Emilie, I'm seventeen years old. The hermit is dead. I loved him.

It wasn't me who found the body. It was the baker's son when he went up with his weekly delivery of bread and provisions. He had been dead for several days. I would have so wanted him to know why I'd stopped coming recently.

It's more than a month since he agreed to tell me his life story. I wrote everything down, the journeys, the jobs, the loves ... On this subject, I tried not to give anything away, but I was quite jealous. Oh, he had loved women! And, to listen to him, they had all left him the fondest memories. One day I couldn't stop myself saying, about one of them:

'If she was really that good, why didn't you stay with her?'

That's when he told me about the little circus. How, in his youth, he had made a journey through a strange labyrinth, looking for the woman of his life and how, at the end of this journey, he had finally given up on this woman. Naturally I asked him why.

'I don't know,' he replied. 'My life would certainly have been just as fine if I had lived with this woman ... But you only have one life and you have to make a choice. I chose to live and die alone ...'

'But you have never been alone!'

'Many women have loved me, that's true ... They've kept me company ... Like you, today, my dear Emilie ... But deep inside I have always remained alone. I have often suffered, but I have also found precious joys in it. For it was what I wanted: to be in dialogue with my shadow ...'

And he took out of his pocket a beautiful polished stone, which he rolled in his hand before putting it back in his jacket.

I didn't know that would be the last time I saw him. I wasn't sure I understood what he was trying to say. I should have gone back, so he could tell me more about it. But immediately after he had told me this story about the little circus, one arrived, the next day, in the village. Normally I'm not interested in this sort of thing, but now all of a sudden I was quite fascinated. As soon as I saw it, in the early afternoon, I stopped to have a look.

Everything was quiet, the people were no doubt having a siesta in their caravans, for it was very hot. I went up to some of the animal cages and stopped in front of the tiger. That's how I met Pablo. He came up behind me, asked jokingly if I wanted him to teach me his trade, for they needed a woman trainer. Oh, Pablo, Pablo with the dark eyes, the white teeth and swarthy skin, I told you I did. That's the first time I'd done that, agree to something just like that. You took me into your caravan and we loved each other straight away.

That evening there was a show and the following day I left with him, with the little circus. I only got back yesterday, at the end of the summer. And I discovered the hermit was dead. I would have so liked to tell him what was happening and to ask his advice. And, above all, to tell him I hadn't abandoned him.

I wonder what he was thinking about at the moment he died. I looked for the stone in his cave, I asked whether it had been discovered on him, but it was nowhere to be found.

The Madman

As soon as I went through the curtain, as soon as I left the little circus, she disappeared. The Shadow of Lost Love. Outside the sunlight was so bright I squinted, then I felt nothing any more, I no longer felt the shadow's hand in mine, I turned round and couldn't see her any more. What was left to me now? The stone, I had given it to her, but they took everything back, my beautiful shadow, the stone, everything. At first, I admit, I thought it wasn't so serious, I barely remembered a thing, I took a couple of steps in the light and already everything was forgotten, I got into my car and drove, I drove very quickly along the road, it was good. It was later that I realized, realized I had nothing left. I loved all those women but not one of them loved me any more, not one of them loved me as I wanted, and I felt so depressed that I stopped everything, anyway I couldn't make love any more, I went to see a woman you pay and it didn't work I felt like lying down in the gutter lying down and flowing away with the water in the gutter. I took drugs and stopped eating meat I rediscovered religion and then stopped I went back to women but they liked me less and less and I didn't even remember the Shadow of Lost Love any more I walked on beaches and gathered stones but I couldn't even remember that she had taken my stone away, oh, why did I want to abduct her? Sometimes I remembered, I looked all over for the little circus, I was like a tramp a vagabond I wandered everywhere looking for it and I finally forgot like always forgot what I was doing but I carried on anyway you have to do something then I stopped and started again women didn't like me any more and I liked them too much. I became a poet and burned everything I became an artist and smashed everything I went mad and I understood everything I grew old and I left, I went to die in the mountains. In the village they told me there was an old hermit in the mountains, a wise old man, so I set off it was a foggy day and the path was arduous, the hermit was waiting for me in front of his door and I saw that he was my double. I want to die I told him die in the mountains and he opened his door to me I went into his cave, he went off somewhere else, went off to live, and I died.

II

The Dead Man

They are all there: my widow and my family with their crocodile tears, my so-called friends, my supposed closest associates and even a representative from the government. A fine cortège behind an empty coffin. Oh, the reckoning up and the backbiting isn't over yet. My inheritance, literal and metaphorical.

They never found my body. The sea swallowed it up.

I soon realized what the mistake, my mistake, was. I should never have taken the Shadow of Myself out of the little circus. That's how I lost her. As soon as I passed through the curtain, she disappeared. Vanished. Later I realized that I had also lost the beautiful polished stone that she had given me.

After this nothing was ever the same as before. Gradually I realized that I had become incapable of loving, that I could no longer feel joyful and carefree. The world disgusted me. I turned to money and power. I amassed as much of both these things that I was able to take from others. The more cynical and contemptuous I became the more women and men tried to win my favour, while still detesting me.

I married a woman who soon had nothing on her mind but divorce and alimony, the best deal she could get from me. But rather than granting her this favour, I had her bear my children, whom neither of us loved. Since I couldn't have pleasure myself, I didn't allow anyone around me to have any.

I treated myself to loads of girls and orgies of every sort. I stocked up on products enabling me to fuck repetitively for hours on end, more and more. I bought a boat. I brought the world's most beautiful women, and the most depraved, to fuck them on this boat. I invented a love story, I invited the woman I had designs on, to love her on this boat. I got erections, I ejaculated a thousand different ways with a thousand different people on this boat. But all to no avail. I never had an orgasm.

One night I left the six bimbos who were slaving away to give me pleasure and went to the bridge. I leaned over the prow of the boat and saw her in the dark water. The Shadow of Myself. I jumped in.

At the bottom of the sea I saw a brightly lit corridor. She was there at the other end. She was waiting for me. My heart was thumping in my chest and I started walking towards her.

I'll soon be there. The corridor is getting darker and darker, but I am sure she is still waiting for me at the end. I hope she is, so much.

The Jugglers

I waited for her at the exit of the little circus, that's how we missed each other the first time. For she was waiting for me too, a short distance away. How we didn't see each other I'll never know. Anyway, we waited for each other, then we both had the same idea: to go to the show that evening.

We didn't see each other there either. It was only after the show that we recognized each other. In the little bar on the other side of the square.

Most of the people from the circus were there too and we hung out with them, because it was a good way for us to get closer to each other, in the general conviviality. At the end of the evening she and I were standing side by side at the bar, laughing together with some of the others. It was a laughter which hid a whole host of things ...

It was very late and everyone was starting to leave. We asked the landlord whether there was a hotel in the village. He said there was one, but it was full. Then the jugglers said, 'Don't worry, little lovebirds, we'll find you a bed.' And they lent us their caravan. That was our first night of love.

And the last, for a long time. She had her bike, I had my car. Before leaving we exchanged telephone numbers written on books of matches. And we lost them. Both of us. I realized I didn't even know her name. I couldn't even look her up in the phone book. As she didn't phone me, I thought she didn't want to see me any more.

A year passed. I had a few flings, but my heart wasn't in it. From time to time I looked at the stone which the Shadow of Myself had given me. And it gave me hope, in love, in myself, in everything.

I thought I had put her out of my mind, but the following summer, when I saw, by chance, that the little circus was performing in a village I was driving through, I stopped. That's where I found her again. She had been passing through too, and had stopped.

From that moment we never left each other. We were both tired of our former lives. We travelled with the circus for a while, where we learned to juggle. We worked out a new act between us, with a touch of something very personal and poetic, which went down very well.

Later we left the circus to try some other things. We had children, grandchildren. Arguments, reconciliations. Happiness, pain. Everything that makes up a life.

This very afternoon we shared a little celebration of love and sex. Play, passion, pleasure ... Once again, with virtuosity we threw back to each other everything we had learned behind the closed doors of the little circus. We are still jugglers ...